years ago, when
Cuba had been
taken out of the oven
to cool and Vietnam
was still coming to
a simmer, Bech did
find a quality of life –
impoverished yet
ceremonial, shabby
yet ornate, sentimental,
embattled, and
avuncular – reminiscent
of his neglected
Jewish past'

JOHN UPDIKE
Born 18 March 1932, Reading, Pennsylvania
Died 27 January 2009, Danvers, Massachusetts

'Foreword', 'Rich in Russia', 'Bech in Rumania', 'Appendix
A' and 'Appendix B' first appeared in book form in *Bech: A
Book* in 1970.

ALSO PUBLISHED BY PENGUIN BOOKS
The Poorhouse Fair · *Rabbit, Run* · *The Centaur* · *Of the Farm* ·
Couples · *Rabbit Redux* · *A Month of Sundays* · *Marry Me* ·
The Coup · *Rabbit is Rich* · *The Witches of Eastwick* · *Roger's
Version* · *S.: A Novel* · *Rabbit at Rest* · *Memories of the Ford
Administration* · *Brazil* · *In the Beauty of the Lilies* · *Toward the
End of Time* · *The Complete Henry Bech* · *The Early Stories* ·
Villages · *Still Looking* · *Terrorist* · *Due Considerations* ·
The Widows of Eastwick · *Endpoint* · *My Father's Tears and
Other Stories*

JOHN UPDIKE

Rich in Russia

PENGUIN BOOKS

PENGUIN CLASSICS

Published by the Penguin Group
Penguin Books Ltd, 80 Strand, London WC2R ORL, England
Penguin Group (USA) Inc., 375 Hudson Street, New York, New York 10014, USA
Penguin Group (Canada), 90 Eglinton Avenue East, Suite 700, Toronto, Ontario,
Canada M4P 2Y3 (a division of Pearson Penguin Canada Inc.)
Penguin Ireland, 25 St Stephen's Green, Dublin 2, Ireland (a division of Penguin Books Ltd)
Penguin Group (Australia), 250 Camberwell Road, Camberwell, Victoria 3124, Australia
(a division of Pearson Australia Group Pty Ltd)
Penguin Books India Pvt Ltd, 11 Community Centre, Panchsheel Park,
New Delhi – 110 017, India
Penguin Group (NZ), 67 Apollo Drive, Rosedale, North Shore 0632, New Zealand
(a division of Pearson New Zealand Ltd)
Penguin Books (South Africa) (Pty) Ltd, 24 Sturdee Avenue, Rosebank, Johannesburg 2196,
South Africa
Penguin Books Ltd, Registered Offices: 80 Strand, London WC2R ORL, England

www.penguin.com

Selected from *Bech: A Book*, first published in 1970 and republished as part of
The Complete Henry Bech in Penguin Classics 1992
This edition published in Penguin Classics 2011

4

Copyright © John Updike, 1970

Typeset by Jouve (UK), Milton Keynes
Printed in England by Clays Ltd, St Ives plc

ISBN: 978-0-141-19625-1

www.greenpenguin.co.uk

Penguin Books is committed to a sustainable future
for our business, our readers and our planet.
The book in your hands is made from paper
certified by the Forest Stewardship Council.

Contents

Foreword

Dear John,

Well, if you must commit the artistic indecency of writing about a writer, better I suppose about me than about you. Except, reading along in these, I wonder if it *is* me, enough me, purely me. At first blush, for example, in Bulgaria (eclectic sexuality, bravura narcissism, thinning curly hair), I sound like some gentlemanly Norman Mailer; then that London glimpse of *silver* hair glints more of gallant, glamorous Bellow, the King of the Leprechauns, than of stolid old homely yours truly. My childhood seems out of Alex Portnoy and my ancestral past out of I. B. Singer. I get a whiff of Malamud in your city breezes, and am I paranoid to feel my 'block' an ignoble version of the more or less noble renunciations of H. Roth, D. Fuchs, and J. Salinger? Withal, something Waspish, theological, scared, and insulatingly ironical that derives, my wild surmise is, from you.

1

Yet you are right. This monotonous hero who disembarks from an aeroplane, mouths words he doesn't quite mean, has vaguely to do with some woman, and gets back on the aeroplane, is certainly one Henry Bech. Until your short yet still not unlongish collection, no revolutionary has concerned himself with our oppression, with the silken mechanism whereby America reduces her writers to imbecility and cozenage. Envied like Negroes, disbelieved in like angels, we veer between the harlotry of the lecture platform and the torture of the writing desk, only to collapse, our five-and-dime Hallowe'en priests' robes a-rustle with economy-class jet-set tickets and honorary certificates from the Cunt-of-the-Month Club, amid a standing crowd of rueful, Lilliputian obituaries. Our language degenerating in the mouths of broadcasters and pop yellers, our formal designs crumbling like sand castles under the feet of beach bullies, we nevertheless and incredibly support with our desperate efforts (just now, I had to look up 'desperate' in the dictionary for the ninety-ninth time, forgetting again if it is spelled with two 'a's or three 'e's) a flourishing culture of publishers, agents, editors, tutors, *Timeniks*, media personnel in all shades of suavity, *chic*, and sexual gusto. When I think of the matings, the moaning, jubilant fornications between ectomorphic oversexed junior editors and svelte hot-from-Wellesley majored-in-

English-minored-in-philosophy female coffee-fetchers and receptionists that have been engineered with the lever of some of my poor scratched-up and pasted-over pages (they arrive in the editorial offices as stiff with Elmer's glue as a masturbator's bedsheet; the office boys use them for tea-trays), I could mutilate myself like sainted Origen, I could keen like Jeremiah. Thank Jahweh these bordellos in the sky can soon dispense with the excuse of us entirely; already the contents of a book count as little as the contents of a breakfast cereal box. It is all a matter of the premium, and the shelf site, and the amount of air between the corn flakes. Never you mind. I'm sure that when with that blithe goyische brass I will never cease to grovel at you approached me for a 'word or two by way of preface', you were bargaining for a benediction, not a curse.

Here it is, then. My blessing. I like some of the things in these accounts very much. The Communists are all good – good *people*. There is a moment by the sea, I've lost the page, that rang true. Here and there passages seem overedited, constipated: you prune yourself too hard. With prose, there is no way to get it out, I have found, but to let it run. I liked some of the women you gave me, and a few of the jokes. By the way, I never – unlike retired light-verse writers – make puns. But if you [*here followed a list of suggested deletions, falsifications,*

3

suppressions, and rewordings, all of which have been scrupulously incorporated – ED.], I don't suppose your publishing this little *jeu* of a book will do either of us drastic harm.

Henry Bech

Manhattan,
4–12 Dec. 1969

Rich in Russia

Students (not unlike yourselves) compelled to buy paperback copies of his novels – notably the first, *Travel Light*, though there has lately been some academic interest in his more surreal and 'existential' and perhaps even 'anarchist' second novel, *Brother Pig* – or encountering some essay from *When the Saints* in a shiny heavy anthology of mid-century literature costing $12.50, imagine that Henry Bech, like thousands less famous than he, is rich. He is not. The paperback rights to *Travel Light* were sold by his publisher outright for two thousand dollars, of which the publisher kept one thousand and Bech's agent one hundred (10 per cent of 50 per cent). To be fair, the publisher had had to remainder a third of the modest hard-cover printing and, when *Travel Light* was enjoying its vogue as the post-Golding pre-Tolkien fad of college undergraduates, would amusingly tell on himself the story of Bech's given-away rights, at sales meetings upstairs in '21'. As to anthologies – the average permissions fee, when it arrives at Bech's mail-box, has been eroded to $64.73, or some such suspiciously odd sum, which barely covers the cost of a restaurant meal with his mistress and a medium wine. Though Bech, and his too numerous interviewers, have made a quixotic virtue of his continuing to live for twenty years in a grim if roomy Riverside Drive apartment building (the mailbox, students should know, where his pitifully nibbled cheques arrive has been well scarred by floating urban wrath, and his last name has been so often ball-pointed by playful lobby-loiterers into a somewhat assonant verb that Bech has left the name plate space blank and depends upon the clairvoyance of mailmen), he in truth lives there because he cannot afford to leave. He was rich just once in his life, and that was in Russia, in 1964, a thaw or so ago.

Russia, in those days, like everywhere else, was a slightly more innocent place. Khruschev, freshly deposed, had left an atmosphere, almost comical, of warmth, of a certain fitful openness, of inscrutable experiment and oblique possibility. There seemed no overweening rea-son why Russia and America, those lovable paranoid giants, could not happily share a globe so big and blue; there certainly seemed no reason why Henry Bech, the recherché but amiable novelist, artistically blocked but socially fluent, should not be flown into Moscow at the expense of our State Department for a month of that mostly imaginary activity termed 'cultural exchange'. Entering the Aeroflot plane at Le Bourget, Bech thought it smelled like his uncles' backrooms in Williamsburg, of swaddled body heat and proximate potatoes boiling.* The impression lingered all month; Russia seemed Jewish to him, and of course he Jewish to Russia. He never knew how much of the tenderness and hospitality he met related to his race. His contact man at the American Embassy – a prissy, doleful ex-basketball-player from Wisconsin, with the all-star name of 'Skip' Reynolds – assured him that two out of every three Soviet intellectuals had suppressed a Jew in their ancestry; and once Bech did find himself in a Moscow apartment whose bookcases were lined with photographs (of Kafka, Einstein, Freud, Wittgenstein) pointedly evoking the glory of pre-Hitlerian *Judenkultur*. His hosts, both man and wife, were professional translators, and the apartment was bewilderingly full of kin, including a doe-eyed young hydraulics engineer and a grandmother who had been a dentist with the Red Army, and whose dental chair dominated the parlour. For a whole

* See Appendix A, section I.

long toasty evening, Jewishness, perhaps also pointedly, was not mentioned. The subject was one Bech was happy to ignore. His own writing had sought to reach out from the ghetto of his heart towards the wider expanses across the Hudson; the artistic triumph of American Jewry lay, he thought, not in the novels of the fifties but in the movies of the thirties, those gargantuan, crass contraptions whereby Jewish brains projected Gentile stars upon a Gentile nation and out of their own immigrant joy gave a formless land dreams and even a kind of conscience. The reservoir of faith, in 1964, was just going dry; through depression and world convulsion the country had been sustained by the *arriviste* patriotism of Louis B. Mayer and the brothers Warner. To Bech, it was one of history's great love stories, the mutually profitable romance between Jewish Hollywood and bohunk America, conducted almost entirely in the dark, a tapping of fervent messages through the wall of the San Gabriel Range; and his favourite Jewish writer was the one who turned his back on his three beautiful Brooklyn novels and went into the desert to write scripts for Doris Day. This may be, except for graduate students, neither here nor there. There, in Russia five years ago, when Cuba had been taken out of the oven to cool and Vietnam was still coming to a simmer, Bech did find a quality of life – impoverished yet ceremonial, shabby yet ornate, sentimental, embattled, and avuncular – reminiscent of his neglected Jewish past. Virtue, in Russia as in his childhood, seemed something that arose from men, like a comforting body odour, rather than something from above, that impaled the struggling soul like a moth on a pin. He stepped from the Aeroflot plane, with its notably hefty stewardesses, into an atmosphere of generosity. They met him with arms heaped with cold roses. On the first afternoon, the Writers' Union gave him as expense money a stack of rouble notes, pink-and-lilac Lenin and powder-blue Spasskaya Tower. In the following month, in the guise of 'royalties' (in honour of his coming they had translated *Travel Light*, and several of his *Commentary* essays ['M-G-M and the U.S.A.'; 'The Moth on the Pin'; 'Daniel Fuchs: An Appreciation'] had appeared in *I Nostrannaya Literatura*, but since no copyright agreements pertained the royalties were arbitrarily calculated, like showers of manna), more roubles were given to him, so that by the week of his departure Bech had accumulated over fourteen hundred roubles – by the official exchange rate, fifteen hundred and forty dollars. There was nothing to spend it on. All his hotels, his plane fares, his meals were paid for. He was a guest of the Soviet state. From morning to night he was never alone. That first afternoon, he had also been given, along with the

9

roubles, a companion, a translator-escort: Ekaterina Alexandrovna Ryleyeva. She was a notably skinny red-headed woman with a flat chest and paper-coloured skin and a translucent wart above her left nostril. He grew to call her Kate.

'Kate,' he said, displaying his roubles in two fistfuls, letting some drift to the floor, 'I have robbed the proletariat. What can I do with my filthy loot?' He had developed, in this long time in which she was always with him, a clowning super-American manner that disguised all complaints as 'acts'. In response, she had strengthened her original pose – of schoolteacherish patience, with ageless peasant roots. Her normal occupation was translating English-language science fiction into Ukrainian, and he imagined this month with him was relatively a holiday. She had a mother, and late at night, after accompanying him to a morning-brandy session with the editors of *Yunost*, to lunch at the Writers' Union with its shark-mouthed chairman,* to Dostoevski's childhood home (next to a madhouse, and enshrining some agonized crosshatched manuscripts and a pair of oval tin spectacles, tiny, as if fashioned for a dormouse), a museum of folk art, an endless restaurant meal, and a night of ballet, Ekaterina would bring

---

* See Appendix A, section II.

Bech to his hotel lobby, put a babushka over her bushy orange hair, and head into a blizzard towards this ailing mother. Bech wondered about Kate's sex life. Skip Reynolds solemnly told him that personal life in Russia was inscrutable. He also told Bech that Kate was undoubtedly a Party spy. Bech was touched, and wondered what in him would be worth spying out. From infancy on we all are spies; the shame is not this but that the secrets to be discovered are so paltry and few. Ekaterina was perhaps as old as forty, which could just give her a lover killed in the war. Was this the secret of her vigil, the endless paper-coloured hours she spent by his side? She was always translating for him, and this added to her neutrality and transparence. He, too, had never been married, and imagined that this was what marriage was like.

She answered, 'Henry' – she usually touched his arm, saying his name, and it never ceased to thrill him a little, the way the 'H' became a breathy guttural sound between 'G' and 'K' – 'you must not joke. This is your money. You earned it by the sweat of your brain. All over Soviet Union committees of people sit in discussion over *Travel Light*, its wonderful qualities. The printing of one hundred thousand copies has gone *poof!* in the bookstores.' The comic-strip colours of science fiction tinted her idiom unexpectedly.

'Poof!' Bech said, and scattered the money above his head; before the last bill stopped fluttering, they both stooped to retrieve the roubles from the rich red carpet. They were in his room at the Sovietskaya, the hotel for Party bigwigs and important visitors; all the suites were furnished in high tsarist style: chandeliers, wax fruit, and brass bears.

'We have banks here,' Kate said shyly, reaching under the satin sofa, 'as in the capitalist countries. They pay interest, you could deposit your money in such a bank. It would be here, enlarged, when you returned. You would have a numbered bankbook.'

'What?' said Bech, 'And help support the Socialist state? When you are already years ahead of us in the space race? I would be adding thrust to your rockets.'

They stood up, both a little breathless from exertion, betraying their age. The tip of her nose was pink. She passed the remainder of his fortune into his hands; her silence seemed embarrassed.

'Besides,' Bech said, 'when would I ever return?'

She offered, 'Perhaps in a space-warp?'

Her shyness, her pink nose and carroty hair, her embarrassment were becoming oppressive. He brusquely waved his arms. 'No, Kate, we must spend it! Spend, spend. It's the Keynesian way. We will make Mother Russia a consumer society.'

From the very still, slightly tipped way she was standing, Bech, bothered by 'space-warp', received a haunted impression – that she was locked into a colourless other dimension from which only the pink tip of her nose emerged. 'Is not so simple,' she ominously pronounced.

For one thing, time was running out. Bobochka and Myshkin, the two Writers' Union officials in charge of Bech's itinerary, had crowded the end of his schedule with compulsory cultural events. Fortified by relatively leisured weeks in Kazakhstan and the Caucasus,* Bech was deemed fit to endure a marathon of war movies (the hero of one of them had lost his Communist Party member's card, which was worse than losing your driver's licence; and in another a young soldier hitched rides in a maze of trains only to turn around at the end ['See, Henry,' Kate whispered to him, 'now he is home, that is his mother, what a good face, so much suffering, now they kiss, now he must leave, oh –' and Kate was crying too much to translate further]) and museums and shrines and brandy with various writers who uniformly adored Gemingway. November was turning bitter, the Christmassy lights celebrating the Revolution had been taken down, Kate as they hurried from appointment to

* See Appendix A, section III.

appointment had developed a sniffle. She constantly patted her nose with a handkerchief. Bech felt a guilty pang, sending her off into the cold towards her mother before he ascended to his luxurious hotel room, with its parqueted foyer stacked with gift books and its alabaster bathroom and its great brocaded double bed. He would drink from a gift bottle of Georgian brandy and stand by the window, looking down on the golden windows of an apartment building where young Russians were Twisting to Voice of America tapes. Chubby Checker's chicken-plucker's voice carried distinctly across the crevasse of sub-arctic night. In an adjoining window, a couple courteously granted isolation by the others was making love; he could see knees and hands and then a rhythmically kicking ankle. To relieve the pressure, Bech would sit down with his brandy and write to distant women boozy reminiscent letters that in the morning would be handed solemnly to the ex-basketball-player, to be sent out of Russia via diplomatic pouch.* Reynolds, himself something of a spy, was with them whenever Bech spoke to a group, as of translators (when asked who was America's best living writer, Bech said Nabokov, and there was quite a silence before the next question) or of students (whom he assured that Yevtushenko's

* See Appendix A, section IV.

Precocious Autobiography was a salubrious and patriotic work that instead of being banned should be distributed free to Soviet schoolchildren). 'Did I put my foot in it?' Bech would ask anxiously afterwards – another 'act'.

The American's careful mouth twitched. 'It's good for them. Shock therapy.'

'You were charming,' Ekaterina Alexandrovna always said loyally, jealously interposing herself, and squeezing Bech's arm. She could not imagine that Bech did not, like herself, loathe all officials. She would not have believed that Bech approached this one with an intellectual's reverence for the athlete, and that they exchanged in private not anti-Kremlin poison but literary gossip and pro football scores, love letters and old copies of *Time*. Now, in her campaign to keep them apart, Kate had been given another weapon. She squeezed his arm smugly and said, 'We have an hour. We must rush off and *shop.*'

For the other thing, there was not much to buy. To begin, he would need an extra suitcase. He and Ekaterina, in their chauffeured Zil, drove to what seemed to Bech a far suburb, past flickerings of birch forest, to sections of new housing, perforated warehouses the colour of wet cement. Here they found a vast store, vast though each salesgirl ruled as a petty tyrant over her domain of shelves. There was a puzzling duplication of suitcase sections; each displayed the same squarish mountain of dark cardboard boxes, and each pouting princess responded with negative insouciance to Ekaterina's quest for a leather suitcase. 'I know there have been some,' she told Bech.

'It doesn't matter,' he said. 'I want a cardboard one. I love the metal studs and the little chocolate handle.'

'You have fun with me,' she said. 'I know what you have in the West. I have been to Science-Fiction Writers' Congress in Vienna. This great store, and not one leather suitcase. It is a disgrace upon the people. But come, I know another store.' They went back into the Zil, which smelled like a cloakroom, and in whose swaying stuffy depths Bech felt squeamish and chastened, having often been sent to the cloakroom as a child at P.S. 87, on West Seventy-seventh Street and Amsterdam Avenue. A dozen stuffy miles and three more stores failed to produce a leather suitcase; at last Kate permitted him to buy a paper one – the biggest, with gay plaid sides, and as long as an oboe. To console her, he also bought an astrakhan hat. It was not flattering (when he put it on, the haughty salesgirl laughed aloud) and did not cover his ears, which were cold, but it had the advantage of costing fifty-four roubles. 'Only a *boyar*,' said Kate, excited to flirtation by his purchase, 'would wear such a wow of a hat.'

'I look like an Armenian in it,' Bech said. Humiliations never come singly. On the street, with his suitcase and hat, Bech was stopped by a man who wanted to buy his overcoat. Kate translated and then scolded. During what Bech took to be a lengthy threat to call the police, the offender, a morose red-nosed man costumed like a New York chestnut vender, stared stubbornly at the sidewalk by their feet.

As they moved away, he said in soft English to Bech, 'Your shoes. I give forty roubles.'

Bech pulled out his wallet and said, '*Nyet, nyet.* For your shoes I give fifty.'

Kate with a squawk flew between them and swept Bech away. She told him in tears, 'Had the authorities witnessed that scene we would all be put in jail, biff, bang.'

Bech had never seen her cry in daylight – only in the dark of projection rooms. He climbed into the Zil feeling especially sick and guilty. They were late for their luncheon, with a cherubic museum director and his hatchet-faced staff. In the course of their tour through the museum, Bech tried to cheer her up with praise of Socialist realism. 'Look at that turbine. Nobody in America can paint a turbine like that. Not since the thirties. Every part so distinct you could rebuild one from it, yet the whole thing romantic as a sunset. Mimesis – you can't beat it.' He was honestly fond of these huge posterish oils; they reminded him of magazine illustrations from his adolescence.

Kate would not be cheered. 'It is stupid stuff,' she said. 'We have had no painters since Rublyov. You treat my country as a picnic.' Sometimes her English had a weird precision. 'It is not as if there is no talent. We are great, there are millions. The young are burning up with talent, it is annihilating them.' She pronounced it *anneeheel* – a word she had met only in print, connected with ray guns.

'Kate, I *mean* it,' Bech insisted, hopelessly in the wrong, as with a third-grade teacher, yet also subject to another pressure, that of a woman taking sensual pleasure in refusing to be consoled. 'I'm telling you, there is artistic passion here. This bicycle. Beautiful impressionism. No spokes. The French paint apples, the Russians paint bicycles.'

The parallel came out awry, unkind. Grimly patting her pink nostrils, Ekaterina passed into the next room. 'Once,' she informed him, 'this room held entirely pictures of *him*. At least that is no more.'

Bech did not need to ask who *he* was. The undefined pronoun had a constant value. In Georgia Bech had been shown a tombstone for a person described simply as Mother.

The next day, between lunch with Voznesensky and dinner with Yevtushenko (who both flatteringly seemed to concede to him a hemispheric celebrity equivalent to their own, and who feigned enchantment when he tried to explain his peculiar status, as not a lion, with a lion's confining burden of symbolic portent, but as a greying, furtively stylish rat indifferently permitted to gnaw and roam behind the wainscoting of a firetrap about to be demolished anyway), he and Kate and the impassive chauffeur managed to buy three amber necklaces and four wooden toys and two very thin wristwatches. The amber seemed homely to Bech – melted butter refrozen – but Kate was proud of it. The wristwatches he suspected would soon stop; they were perilously thin. The toys – segmented Kremlins, carved bears chopping wood – were good, but the only children he knew were his sister's in Cincinnati, and the youngest was nine. The Ukrainian needlework that Ekaterina hopefully pushed at him his imagination could not impose on any woman he knew, not even his mother; since his 'success', she had her hair done once a week and wore her hems just above the knee. Back in his hotel room, in the ten minutes before an all-Shostakovich concert, while Kate sniffed and sloshed in the bathroom (how could such a skinny woman be displacing all that water?), Bech counted his roubles. He had spent only a hundred and thirty-seven. That left one thousand two hundred and eighty-three, plus the odd kopecks. His heart sank; it was hopeless. Ekaterina emerged from the bathroom with a strange, bruised stare. Little burnt traces, traces of ashen tears, lingered about her eyes, which were by nature a washed-out blue. She had been trying to put on eye makeup, and had kept washing it off. Trying to be a rich man's wife. She looked blank and wounded. Bech took her arm; they hurried downstairs like criminals on the run.

The next day was his last full day in Russia. All month he had wanted to visit Tolstoy's estate, and the trip had been postponed until now. Since Yasnaya Polyana was four hours from Moscow, he and Kate left early in the morning and returned in the dark. After miles of sleepy silence, she asked, 'Henry, what did you like?'

'I liked the way he wrote *War and Peace* in the cellar, *Anna Karenina* on the first floor, and *Resurrection* upstairs. Do you think he's writing a fourth novel in Heaven?'

This reply, taken from a little *Commentary* article he was writing in his head (and would never write on paper), somehow renewed her silence. When she at last spoke, her voice was shy. 'As a Jew, you believe?'

His laugh had an ambushed quality he tried to translate, with a shy guffaw at the end, into self-deprecation. 'Jews don't go in much for Paradise,' he said. 'That's something you Christians cooked up.'

'We are not Christians.'

'Kate, you are saints. You are a land of monks and your government is a constant penance.' From the same unwritten article – tentatively titled 'God's Ghost in Moscow'. He went on, with Hollywood, Martin Buber, and his uncles all vaguely smiling in his mind, 'I think the Jewish feeling is that wherever they happen to be, it's rather paradisiacal, because they're there.'

'You have found it so here?'

'Very much. This must be the only country in the world you can be homesick for while you're still in it. Russia is one big case of homesickness.'

Perhaps Kate found this ground dangerous, for she returned to earlier terrain. 'It is strange,' she said, 'of the books I translate, how much there is to do with supernature. Immaterial creatures like angels, ideal societies composed of spirits, speeds that exceed that of light, reversals of time – all impossible, and perhaps not. In a way it is terrible to look up at the sky, on one of our clear nights of burning cold, at the sky of stars, and think of creatures alive in it.'

'Like termites in the ceiling.' Falling so short of the grandeur Kate might have had a right to expect from him, his simile went unanswered. The car swayed, dark gingerbread villages swooped by, the back of the driver's head was motionless. Bech idly hummed a bit of 'Midnight in Moscow', whose literal title, he had discovered, was 'Twilit Evenings in the Moscow Suburbs'. He said, 'I also liked the way Upton Sinclair was in his bookcase, and how his house felt like a farmhouse instead of a mansion, and his grave.'

'So super a grave.'

'Very graceful, for a man who fought death so hard.' It had been an unmarked oval of earth, rimmed green with frozen turf, at the end of a road in a birchwood where night was sifting in. It had been here that Tolstoy's brother had told him to search for the little green stick that would end war and human suffering. Because her importunate silence had begun to nag unbearably, Bech told Kate, 'That's what I should do with my roubles. Buy Tolstoy a tombstone. With a neon arrow.'

'Oh those roubles!' she exclaimed. 'You persecute me with those roubles. We have shopped more in one week than I shop in one year. Material things do not interest me, Henry. In the war we all learned the value of material things. There is no value but what you hold within yourself.'

'O.K., I'll swallow them.'

'Always the joke. I have one more desperate idea. In New York, you have women for friends?'

Her voice had gone shy, as when broaching Jewishness; she was asking him if he were a homosexual. How little, after a month, these two knew each other! 'Yes, I have *only* women for friends.'

'Then perhaps we could buy them some furs. Not a

coat, the style would be wrong. But fur we have, not leather suitcases, no, you are right to mock us, but furs, the world's best, and dear enough for even a man so rich as you. I have often argued with Bobochka, he says authors should be poor for the suffering, it is how capitalist countries do it; and now I see he is right.'

Astounded by this tirade, delivered with a switching head so that her mole now and then darted into translucence – for they had reached Moscow's outskirts, and street lamps – Bech could only say, 'Kate, you've never read my books. They're *all* about women.'

'Yes,' she said, 'but coldly observed. As if extraterrestrial life.'

To be brief (I saw you, in the back row, glancing at your wristwatch, and don't think that glance will sweeten your term grade), fur it was. The next morning, in a scrambled hour before the ride to the airport, Bech and Ekaterina went to a shop on Gorky Street where a diffident Mongolian beauty laid pelt after pelt into his hands. The less unsuccessful of his uncles had been for a time a furrier, and after this gap of decades Bech again greeted the frosty luxuriance of silver fox, the more tender and playful and amorous amplitude of red fox, mink with its ugly mahogany assurance, svelte otter, imperial ermine tail-tipped in black like a writing plume. Each pelt, its soft tingling mass condensing acres of Siberia, cost several hundred roubles. Bech bought for his mother two mink still wearing their dried snarls, and two silver fox for his present mistress, Norma Latchett, to trim a coat collar in (her firm white Saxon chin *drowned* in fur, is how he pictured it), and some ermine as a joke for his house-slave sister in Cincinnati, and a sumptuous red fox for a woman he had yet to meet. The Mongolian salesgirl, magnificently unimpressed, added it up to over twelve hundred roubles and wrapped the furs in brown paper like fish. He paid her with a salad of pastel notes and was clean. Bech had not been so exhilarated, so aerated by prosperity, since he sold his first short story – in 1943, about boot camp, to *Liberty*, for a hundred and fifty dollars. It had been humorous, a New York Jew floundering among Southerners, and is omitted from most bibliographies.*

He and Ekaterina rushed back to the Sovietskaya and completed his packing. He tried to forget the gift books stacked in the foyer, but she insisted he take them. They crammed them into his new suitcase, with the furs, the amber, the wristwatches, the infuriatingly knobby and bulky wooden toys. When they were done, the suitcase bulged, leaked fur, and weighed more than his two others

* See Appendix B.

combined. Bech looked his last at the chandelier and the empty brandy bottle, the lovesick window and the bugged walls, and staggered out the door. Kate followed with a book and a sock she had found beneath the bed.

Everyone was at the airport to see him off – Bobochka with his silver teeth, Myshkin with his glass eye, the rangy American with his air of lugubrious caution. Bech shook Skip Reynolds's hand good-bye and abrasively kissed the two Russian men on the cheek. He went to kiss Ekaterina on the cheek, but she turned her face so that her mouth met his and he realized, horrified, that he should have slept with her. He had been expected to. From the complacent tiptoe smiles of Bobochka and Myshkin, they assumed he had. She had been provided to him for that purpose. He was a guest of the state. 'Oh Kate, forgive me; of course,' he said, but so stumblingly she seemed not to have understood him. Her kiss had been colourless but moist and good, like a boiled potato.

Then, somehow, suddenly, he was late, there was panic. His suitcases were not yet in the aeroplane. A brute in blue seized the two manageable ones and left him to carry the paper one himself. As he staggered across the runway, it burst. One catch simply tore loose at the staples, and the other sympathetically let go. The books and toys spilled; the fur began to blow down the concrete, pelts looping and shimmering as if again alive.

Kate broke past the gate guard and helped him catch them; together they scooped all the loot back in the suitcase, but for a dozen fluttering books. They were heavy and slick, in the Cyrillic alphabet, like high-school yearbooks upside down. One of the watches had cracked its face. Kate was sobbing and shivering in excitement; a bitter wind was blowing streaks of grit and snow out of the coming long winter. 'Genry, the books!' she said, needing to shout. 'You must have them! They are souvenirs!'

'Mail them!' Bech thundered, and ran with the terrible suitcase under his arm, fearful of being burdened with more responsibilities. Also, though in some ways a man of our time, he has a morbid fear of missing aeroplanes, and of being dropped from the tail-end lavatory.

Though this was five years ago, the books have not yet arrived in the mail. Perhaps Ekaterina Alexandrovna kept them, as souvenirs. Perhaps they were caught in the cultural freeze-up that followed Bech's visit, and were buried in a blizzard. Perhaps they arrived in the lobby of his apartment building, and were pilfered by an émigré vandal. Or perhaps (you may close your notebooks) the mailman is not clairvoyant after all.

Bech in Rumania
or, The Rumanian Chauffeur

Deplaning in Bucharest wearing an astrakhan hat purchased in Moscow, Bech was not recognized by the United States Embassy personnel sent to greet him, and, rather than identify himself, sat sullenly on a bench, glowering like a Soviet machinery importer while these young men ran back and forth conversing with each other in dismayed English and shouting at the customs officials in what Bech took to be pidgin Rumanian. At last, one of these young men, the smallest and cleverest, Princeton '51 or so, noticing the rounded toes of Bech's American shoes, ventured suspiciously 'I beg your pardon, *pazhalusta*, but arc you – ?'

'Could be,' Bech said. After five weeks of consorting with Communists, he felt himself increasingly tempted to evade, confuse, and mock his fellow Americans. Further, after attuning himself to the platitudinous jog of translatorese, he found rapid English idiom exhausting. So it was with some relief that he passed, in the next hours, from the conspiratorial company of his compatriots into the care of a monarchial Rumanian hotel and a smiling Party underling called Athanase Petrescu.

Petrescu, whose oval face was adorned by constant sunglasses and several round sticking plasters placed upon a fresh blue shave, had translated into Rumanian *Typee, Pierre, Life on the Mississippi, Sister Carrie, Winesburg, Ohio, Across the River and Into the Trees*, and *On the Road*. He knew Bech's work well and said, 'Although it was *Travel Light* that made your name illustrious, yet in my heart I detect a very soft spot for *Brother Pig*, which your critics did not so much applaud.'

Bech recognized in Petrescu, behind the blue jaw and sinister glasses, a man humbly in love with books, a fool for literature. As, that afternoon, they strolled through a dreamlike Bucharest park containing bronze busts of Goethe and Pushkin and Victor Hugo, beside a lake wherein the greenish sunset was coated with silver, the translator talked excitedly of a dozen things, sharing thoughts he had not been able to share while descending, alone at his desk, into the luminous abysses and profound crudities of American literature. 'With Hemingway, the difficulty of translating – and I speak to an extent of Anderson also – is to prevent the simplicity from seeming simple-minded. For we do not have here such a tradition of belle-lettrist fancifulness against which the style of Hemingway was a rebel. Do you follow the difficulty?'

'Yes. How did you get around it?'

Petrescu did not seem to understand. 'Get around, how? Circumvent?'

'How did you translate the simple language without seeming simple-minded?'

'Oh. By being extremely subtle.'

'Oh. I should tell you, some people in my country think Hemingway *was* simple-minded. It is actively debated.'

Petrescu absorbed this with a nod, and said, 'I know for a fact, his Italian is not always correct.'

When Bech got back to his hotel – situated on a square rimmed with buildings made, it seemed, of dusty pink candy – a message had been left for him to call Phillips at the U.S. Embassy. Phillips was Princeton '51. He asked, 'What have they got mapped out for you?'

Bech's schedule had hardly been discussed. 'Petrescu mentioned a production of *Desire Under the Elms* I might see. And he wants to take me to Braşov. Where is Braşov?'

'In Transylvania, way the hell off. It's where Dracula hung out. Listen, can we talk frankly?'

'We can try.'

'I know damn well this line is bugged, but here goes. This country is hot. Anti-Socialism is bursting out all over. My inkling is they want to get you out of Bucharest, away from all the liberal writers who are dying to meet you.'

'Are you sure they're not dying to meet Arthur Miller?'

'Kidding aside, Bech, there's a lot of ferment in this country, and we want to plug you in. Now, when are you meeting Taru?'

'Knock knock. Taru. Taru Who?'

'Jesus, he's the head of the Writer's Union – hasn't Petrescu even set up an appointment? Boy, they're putting you right around the old mulberry bush. I gave Petrescu a list of writers for you to latch on to. Suppose I call him and wave the big stick and ring you back. Got it?'

'Got it, tiger.' Bech hung up sadly; one of the reasons he had accepted the State Department's invitation was that he thought it would be an escape from agents.

Within ten minutes his phone rasped, in that dead rattly way it has behind the Iron Curtain, and it was Phillips, breathless, victorious. 'Congratulate me,' he said. 'I've been making like a thug and got *their* thugs to give you an appointment with Taru tonight.'

'This very night?'

Phillips sounded hurt. 'You're only here four nights, you know. Petrescu will pick you up. His excuse was he thought you might want some rest.'

'He's extremely subtle.'

'What was that?'

'Never mind, *pazhalusta*.'

Petrescu came for Bech in a black car driven by a hunched silhouette. The Writers' Union was housed on the other side of town, in a kind of castle, a turreted mansion with a flaring stone staircase and an oak-vaulted library whose shelves were twenty feet high and solid with leather spines. The stairs and chambers seemed deserted. Petrescu tapped on a tall panelled door of blackish oak, strap-hinged in the sombre Spanish style. The door soundlessly opened, revealing a narrow high room hung with tapestries, pale brown and blue, whose subject involved masses of attenuated soldiery unfathomably engaged. Behind a huge polished desk quite bare of furnishings sat an immaculate miniature man with a pink face and hair as white as a dandelion poll. His rosy hands, perfectly finished down to each fingernail, were folded on the shiny desk, reflected like water flowers; and his face wore a smiling expression that was also, in each neat crease, beyond improvement. This was Taru.

He spoke with magical suddenness, like a music box.

Petrescu translated his words to Bech as, 'You are a literary man. Do you know the works of our Mihail Sadoveanu, of our noble Mihai Beniuc, or perhaps that most wonderful spokesman for the people, Tudor Arghezi?'

Bech said, 'No, I'm afraid the only Rumanian writer I know at all is Ionesco.'

The exquisite white-haired man nodded eagerly and emitted a length of tinkling sounds that was translated to Bech as simply 'And who is he?'

Petrescu, who certainly knew all about Ionesco, stared at Bech with blank expectance. Even in this innermost sanctum he had kept his sunglasses on. Bech said, irritated, 'A playwright. Lives in Paris. Theatre of the Absurd. Wrote *Rhinoceros*,' and he crooked a forefinger beside his heavy Jewish nose, to represent a horn.

Taru emitted a dainty sneeze of laughter. Petrescu translated, listened, and told Bech, 'He is very sorry he has not heard of this man. Western books are a luxury here, so we are not able to follow each new nihilist movement. Comrade Taru asks what you plan to do while in the People's Republic of Rumania.'

'I am told,' Bech said, 'that there are some writers interested in exchanging ideas with an American colleague. I believe my embassy has suggested a list to you.'

The musical voice went on and on. Petrescu listened with a cocked ear and relayed, 'Comrade Taru sincerely wishes that this may be the case and regrets that, because of the lateness of the hour and the haste of this meeting urged by your embassy, no secretaries are present to locate this list. He furthermore regrets that at this time of the year so many of our fine writers are bathing at the Black Sea. However, he points out that there is an excellent production of *Desire Under the Elms* in Bucharest, and that our Carpathian city of Braşov is indeed worthy of a visit. Comrade Taru himself retains many pleasant youthful memories concerning Braşov.'

Taru rose to his feet – an intensely dramatic event within the reduced scale he had established around himself. He spoke, thumped his small square chest resoundingly, spoke again, and smiled. Petrescu said, 'He wishes you to know that in his youth he published many books of poetry, both epic and lyric in manner. He adds, "A fire ignited here"' – and here Petrescu struck his own chest in flaccid mimicry – '"can never be quenched."'

Bech stood and responded, 'In my country we also ignite fires *here*.' He touched his head. His remark was not translated and, after an efflorescent display of courtesy from the brilliant-haired little man, Bech and Petrescu made their way through the empty mansion down to the waiting car, which drove them, rather jerkily, back to the hotel.

'And how did you like Mr Taru?' Petrescu asked on the way.

'He's a doll,' Bech said.

'You mean – a puppet?'

Bech turned curiously but saw nothing in Petrescu's face that betrayed more than a puzzlement over meaning. Bech said, 'I'm sure you have a better eye for the strings than I do.'

Since neither had eaten, they dined together at the hotel; they discussed Faulkner and Hawthorne while waiters brought them soup and veal a continent removed from the cabbagy cuisine of Russia. A lithe young woman on awkwardly high heels stalked among the tables singing popular songs from Italy and France. The trailing microphone wire now and then became entangled in her feet, and Bech admired the sly savagery with which she would, while not altering an iota her enamelled smile, kick herself free. Bech had been a long time without a woman. He looked forward to three more nights sitting at this table, surrounded by travelling salesmen from East Germany and Hungary, feasting on the sight of this lithe chanteuse. Though her motions were angular and her smile was inflexible, her high round bosom looked soft as a soufflé.

But tomorrow, Petrescu explained, smiling sweetly beneath his sad-eyed sunglasses, they would go to Braşov.

Bech knew little about Rumania. From his official briefing he knew it was 'a Latin island in a Slavic sea', that during World War II its anti-Semitism had been the most ferocious in Europe, that now it was seeking economic independence of the Soviet bloc. The ferocity especially interested him, since of the many human conditions it was his business to imagine, murderousness was among the more difficult. He was a Jew. Though he could be irritable and even vengeful, obstinate savagery was excluded from his budget of emotions.

Petrescu met him in the hotel lobby at nine and, taking his suitcase from his hand, led him to the hired car. By daylight, the chauffeur was a short man the colour of ashes – white ash for the face, grey cigarette ash for his close-trimmed smudge of a moustache, and the darker residue of a tougher substance for his eyes and hair. His manner was nervous and remote and fussy; Bech's impression was of a stupidity so severe that the mind is tensed to sustain the simplest tasks. As they drove from the city, the driver constantly tapped his horn to warn pedestrians and cyclists of his approach. They passed the prewar stucco suburbs, suggestive of southern California;

the postwar Moscow-style apartment buildings, rectilinear and airless; the heretical all-glass exposition halls the Rumanians had built to celebrate twenty years of industrial progress under Socialism. It was shaped like a huge sailor's cap, and before it stood a tall Brancusi column cast in aluminium.

'Brancusi,' Bech said. 'I didn't know you acknowledged him.'

'Oh, much,' Petrescu said. 'His village is a shrine. I can show you many early works in our national museum.'

'And Ionesco? Is he really a non-person?'

Petrescu smiled. 'The eminent head of our Writers' Union,' he said, 'makes little jokes. He is known here but not much produced as yet. Students in their rooms perhaps read aloud a play like *The Singer Devoid of Hair.*'

Bech was distracted from the conversation by the driver's incessant mutter of tooting. They were in the country now, driving along a straight, slightly rising road lined with trees whose trunks were painted white. On the shoulder of the road walked bundle-shaped old women carrying knotted bundles, little boys tapping donkeys forward, men in French-blue work clothes sauntering empty-handed. At all of them the driver sounded his horn. His stubby, grey-nailed hand fluttered on the contact rim, producing an agitated stammer beginning perhaps a hundred yards in advance and continuing until the person, who usually moved only to turn and scowl, had been passed. Since the road was well travelled, the noise was practically uninterrupted, and after the first half hour nagged Bech like a toothache. He asked Petrescu, 'Must he do that?'

'Oh, yes. He is a conscientious man.'

'What good does it do?'

Petrescu, who had been developing an exciting thought on Mark Twain's infatuation with the apparatus of capitalism, which had undermined his bucolic genius, indulgently explained, 'The bureau from which we hire cars provides the driver. They have been precisely trained for this profession.'

Bech realized that Petrescu himself did not drive. He reposed in the oblivious trust of an aeroplane passenger, legs crossed, sunglasses in place, issuing smoother and smoother phrases, while Bech leaned forward anxiously, braking on the empty floor, twitching a wheel that was not there, trying to wrench the car's control away from this atrociously unrhythmic and brutal driver. When they went through a village, the driver would speed up and intensify the mutter of his honking; clusters of peasants and geese exploded in disbelief, and Bech felt as if gears, the gears that space and engage the mind, were clashing. As they ascended into the mountains, the driver demonstrated his technique with curves: he approached each like an enemy, accelerating, and at the last moment stepped on the brake as if crushing a snake underfoot. In the jerking and swaying, Petrescu grew pale. His blue jaw acquired a moist sheen and issued phrases less smoothly. Bech said to him, 'This driver should be locked up. He is sick and dangerous.'

'No, no, he is a good man. These roads, they are difficult.'

'At least please ask him to stop twiddling the horn. It's torture.'

Petrescu's eyebrows arched, but he leaned forward and spoke in Rumanian.

The driver answered; the language clattered in his mouth, though his voice was soft.

Petrescu told Bech, 'He says it is a safety precaution.'

'Oh, for Christ's sake!'

Petrescu was truly puzzled. He asked, 'In the States, you drive your own car?'

'Of course, everybody does,' Bech said, and then worried that he had hurt the feelings of this Socialist, who must submit to the aristocratic discomfort of being driven. For the remainder of the trip, he held silent about the driver. The muddy lowland fields with Mediterranean farmhouses had yielded to fir-dark hills bearing Germanic chalets. At the highest point, the old boundary of Austria-Hungary, fresh snow had fallen, and the car, pressed ruthlessly through the ruts, brushed within inches of some children dragging sleds. It was a short downhill distance from there to Braşov. They stopped before a newly built pistachio hotel. The jarring ride had left Bech with a headache. Petrescu stepped carefully from the car, licking his lips; the tip of his tongue showed purple in his drained face. The chauffeur, as composed as raked ashes no touch of wind has stirred, changed out of his grey driving coat, checked the oil and water, and removed his lunch from the trunk. Bech examined him for some sign of satisfaction, some betraying trace of malice, but there was nothing. His eyes were living smudges, and his mouth was the mouth of the boy in the class who, being neither strong nor intelligent, has developed insignificance into a positive character trait that does him some credit. He glanced at Bech without expression; yet Bech wondered if the man did not understand English a little.

In Braşov the American writer and his escort passed the time in harmless sightseeing. The local museum contained peasant costumes. The local castle contained armour. The Lutheran cathedral was surprising; Gothic lines and scale had been wedded to clear glass and an austerity of decoration, noble and mournful, that left one, Bech felt, much too alone with God. He felt the Reformation here as a desolating wind, four hundred years ago. From the hotel roof, the view looked sepia, and there was an empty swimming pool, and wet snow on the lacy metal chairs. Petrescu shivered and went down to his room. Bech changed neckties and went down to the bar. Champagne music bubbled from the walls. The bartender understood what a Martini was, though he used equal parts of gin and vermouth. The clientele was young, and many spoke Hungarian, for Transylvania had been taken from Hungary after the war. One plausible youth, working with Bech's reluctant French, elicited from him that he was *un écrivain*, and asked for his autograph. But this turned out to be the prelude to a proposed exchange of pens, in which Bech lost a sentimentally cherished Esterbrook and gained a nameless ball-point that wrote red. Bech wrote three and a half postcards (to his mistress, his mother, his publisher, and a half to his editor at *Commentary*) before the red pen went dry. Petrescu, who neither drank nor smoked, finally appeared. Bech said, 'My hero, where have you been? I've had four Martinis and been swindled in your absence.'

Petrescu was embarrassed. 'I've been shaving.'

'Shaving!'

'Yes, it is humiliating. I must spend each day one hour shaving, and even yet it does not look as if I have shaved, my beard is so obdurate.'

'Are you putting blades in the razor?'

'Oh, yes, I buy the best and use two upon each occasion.'

'This is the saddest story I've ever heard. Let me send you some decent blades when I get home.'

'Please, do not. There are no blades better than the blades I use. It is merely that my beard is phenomenal.'

'When you die,' Bech said, 'you can leave it to Rumanian science.'

'You are ironical.'

In the restaurant, there was dancing – the Tveest, the Hully Gullee, and chain formations that involved a lot of droll hopping. American dances had become here innocently birdlike. Now and then a young man, slender and with hair combed into a parrot's peak, would leap into the air and seem to hover, emitting a shrill palatal cry. The men in Rumania appeared lighter and more fanciful than the women, who moved, in their bell-skirted cocktail dresses, with a wooden stateliness perhaps inherited from their peasant grandmothers.

Each girl who passed near their table was described by Petrescu, not humorously at first, as a 'typical Rumanian beauty'.

'And this one, with the orange lips and eyelashes?'

'A typical Rumanian beauty. The cheekbones are very classical.'

'And the blonde behind her? The small plump one?'

'Also typical.'

'But they are so different. Which is more typical?'

'They are equally. We are a perfect democracy.' Between spates of dancing, a young chanteuse, more talented than the one in the Bucharest hotel, took the floor. She had learned, probably from free-world films, that terrible mannerism of strenuousness whereby every note, no matter how accessibly placed and how flatly attacked, is given a facial aura of immense accomplishment. Her smile, at the close of each number, triumphantly combined a conspiratorial twinkle, a sublime humility, and the dazed self-congratulation of post-coital euphoria. Yet, beneath the artifice, the girl had life. Bech was charmed by a number, in Italian, that involved much animated pouting and finger-scolding and placing of the fists on the hips. Petrescu explained that the song was the plaint of a young wife whose husband was always attending soccer matches and never stayed home with her. Bech asked, 'Is she also a typical Rumanian beauty?'

'I think,' Petrescu said, with a purr Bech had not heard before, 'she is a typical little Jewess.'

The drive, late the next afternoon, back to Bucharest was worse than the one out, for it took place partly in the dark. The chauffeur met the challenge with increased speed and redoubled honking. In a rare intermittence of danger, a straight road near Ploesti where only the oil rigs relieved the flatness, Bech asked, 'Seriously, do you not feel the insanity in this man?' Five minutes before, the driver had turned to the back seat and, showing even grey teeth in a tight tic of a smile, had remarked about a dog lying dead beside the road. Bech suspected that most of the remark had not been translated.

Petrescu said, crossing his legs in the effete and weary way that had begun to exasperate Bech, 'No, he is a good man, an extremely kind man, who takes his work too seriously. In that he is like the beautiful Jewess whom you so much admired.'

'In my country,' Bech said, '"Jewess" is a kind of fighting word.'

'Here,' Petrescu said, 'it is merely descriptive. Let us talk about Herman Melville. Is it possible to you that *Pierre* is a yet greater work than *The White Whale*?'

'No, I think it is yet not so great, possibly.'

'You are ironical about my English. Please excuse it.

43

Being prone to motion sickness has discollected my thoughts.'

'Our driver would discollect anybody's thoughts. Is it possible that he is the late Adolf Hitler, kept alive by Count Dracula?'

'I think not. Our people's uprising in 1944 fortunately exterminated the Fascists.'

'That is fortunate. Have you ever read, speaking of Melville, *Omoo*?'

Melville, it happened, was Bech's favourite American author, in whom he felt united the strengths that were later to go the separate ways of Dreiser and James. Throughout dinner, back at the hotel, he lectured Petrescu about him. 'No one,' Bech said – he had ordered a full bottle of white Rumanian wine, and his tongue felt agile as a butterfly – 'more courageously faced our native terror. He went for it right between its wide-set little pig eyes, and it shattered his genius like a lance.' He poured himself more wine. The hotel chanteuse, who Bech now noticed had buck teeth as well as gawky legs, stalked to their table, untangled her feet from the microphone wire, and favoured them with a French version of 'Some Enchanted Evening'.

'You do not consider,' Petrescu said, 'that Hawthorne also went between the eyes? And the laconic Ambrose Bierce?'

'*Quelque soir enchanté,*' the girl sang, her eyes and teeth and earrings glittering like the facets of a chandelier.

'Hawthorne blinked,' Bech pronounced, 'and Bierce squinted.'

'*Vous verrez l'étranger . . .*'

'I worry about you, Petrescu,' Bech continued. 'Don't you ever have to go home? Isn't there a Frau Petrescu, Madame, or whatever, a typical Rumanian, never mind.' Abruptly he felt steeply lonely.

In bed, when his room had stopped the gentle swaying motion with which it had greeted his entrance, he remembered the driver, and the man's neatly combed death-grey face seemed the face of everything foul, stale, stupid, and uncontrollable in the world. He had seen that tight tic of a smile before. Where? He remembered. West Eighty-sixth Street, coming back from Riverside Park, a childhood playmate, with whom he always argued, and was always right, and always lost. Their ugliest quarrel had concerned comic strips, whether or not the artist – Segar, say, who drew Popeye, or Harold Gray of Little Orphan Annie – whether or not the artist, in duplicating the faces from panel to panel, day after day, traced them. Bech had maintained, obviously, not. The other boy had insisted that some mechanical process was used. Bech tried to explain that it was not such a difficult

45

feat, that just as one's handwriting is always the same –
The other boy, his face clouding, said it wasn't possible.
Bech explained, what he felt so clearly, that everything
was possible for human beings, with a little training and
talent, that the ease and variation of each panel proved –
The other face had become totally closed, with a density
quite inhuman, as it steadily shook 'No, no, no', and
Bech, becoming frightened and furious, tried to behead
the other boy with his fists, and the boy in turn pinned
him and pressed his face into the bitter grits of pebble
and glass that coated the cement passageway between
two apartment buildings. These unswept jagged bits, a
kind of city topsoil, had enlarged under his eyes, and
this experience, the magnification amidst pain of those
negligible mineral flecks, had formed, perhaps, a vision.
At any rate, it seemed to Bech, as he skidded into sleep,
that his artistic gifts had been squandered in the attempt
to recapture that moment of stinging precision.

The next day was his last full day in Rumania. Petrescu
took him to an art museum where, amid many ethnic
posters posing as paintings, a few sketches and sculpted
heads by the young Brancusi smelled like saints' bones.
The two men went on to the twenty years' industrial
exhibit and admired rows of brightly painted machinery – gaudy counters in some large international game.

They visited shops, and everywhere Bech felt a desiccated pinkish elegance groping, out of eclipse, through the murky hardware of Sovietism, towards a rebirth of style. Yet there had been a tough and heroic naïveté in Russia that he missed here, where something shrugging and effete seemed to leave room for a vein of energetic evil. In the evening, they went to *Patima de Sub Ulmi*.

Their driver, bringing them to the very door of the theatre, pressed his car forward through bodies, up an arc of driveway crowded with pedestrians. The people caught in the headlights were astonished; Bech slammed his foot on a phantom brake and Petrescu grunted and strained backwards in his seat. The driver continually tapped his horn – a demented, persistent muttering – and slowly the crowd gave way around the car. Bech and Petrescu stepped, at the door, into the humid atmosphere of a riot. As the chauffeur, his childish small-nosed profile intent, pressed his car back through the crowd to the street, fists thumped on the fenders.

Safe in the theatre lobby, Petrescu took off his sunglasses to wipe his face. His eyes were a tender bulging blue, with jaundiced whites; a scholar's tremor pulsed in his left lower lid. 'You know,' he confided to Bech, 'that man our driver. Not all is well with him.'

'Could be,' Bech said.

O'Neill's starveling New England farmers were

played as Russian muzhiks; they wore broad-belted coats and high black boots and kept walloping each other on the back. Abbie Cabot had become a typical Rumanian beauty, ten years past prime, with a beauty spot on one cheek and artful bare arms as supple as a swan's neck. Since their seats were in the centre of the second row, Bech had a good if infrequent view down the front of her dress, and thus, ignorant of when the plot would turn her his way, he contentedly manufactured suspense for himself. But Petrescu, his loyalty to American letters affronted beyond endurance, insisted that they leave after the first act. 'Wrong, wrong,' he complained. 'Even the pitchforks were wrong.'

'I'll have the State Department send them an authentic American pitchfork,' Bech promised.

'And the girl – the girl is not like that, not a coquette. She is a religious innocent, under economic stress.'

'Well, scratch an innocent, find a coquette.'

'It is your good nature to joke, but I am ashamed you saw such a travesty. Now our driver is not here. We are undone.'

The street outside the theatre, so recently jammed, was empty and dark. A solitary couple walked slowly towards them. With surrealist suddenness, Petrescu fell into the arms of the man, walloping his back, and then kissed the calmly proffered hand of the woman. The couple was introduced to Bech as 'a most brilliant young writer and his notably ravishing wife'. The man, stolid and forbidding, wore rimless glasses and a bulky checked topcoat. The woman was scrawny; her face, potentially handsome, had been worn to its bones by the nervous stress of intelligence. She had a cold and a command, quick but limited, of English. 'Are you having a liking for this?' she asked.

Bech understood her gesture to include all Rumania. 'Very much,' he answered. 'After Russia, it seems very civilized.'

'And who isn't?' she snapped. 'What are you liking most?'

Petrescu roguishly interposed, 'He has a passion for night-club singers.'

The wife translated this to her husband; he took his hands from his overcoat pockets and clapped them. He was wearing leather gloves, so the noise was loud on the deserted street. He spoke, and Petrescu translated, 'He says we should therefore, as hosts, escort you to the most celebrated night club in Bucharest, where you will see many singers, each more glorious than the preceding.'

'But,' Bech said, 'weren't they going somewhere? Shouldn't they go home?' It worried him that Communists never seemed to go home.

'For why?' the wife cried.

'You have a cold,' Bech told her. Her eyes didn't comprehend. He touched his own nose, so much larger than hers. *'Un rhume.'*

'Poh!' she said. 'Itself takes care of tomorrow.'

The writer owned a car, and he drove them, with the gentleness of a pedal boat, through a maze of alleys overhung by cornices suggestive of cake frosting, of waves breaking, of seashells, lion paws, unicorn horns, and cumulus clouds. They parked across the street from a blue sign, and went into a green doorway, and down a yellow set of stairs. Music approached them from one direction and a coat-check girl in net tights from the other. It was to Bech as if he were dreaming of an American night club, giving it the strange spaciousness of dreams. The main room had been conjured out of several basements – a cave hollowed from the underside of jeweller's shops and vegetable marts. Tables were set in shadowy tiers arranged around a central square floor. Here a man with a red wig and mascaraed eyes was talking into a microphone, mincingly. Then he sang, in the voice of a choirboy castrated too late. A waiter materialized. Bech ordered Scotch, the other writer ordered vodka. The wife asked for cognac and Petrescu for mineral water. Three girls dressed as rather naked bicyclists appeared with a dwarf on a unicycle and did some unsmiling gyrations to music while he pedalled among them, tugging bows and displacing straps. 'Typical Polish beauties,' Petrescu explained in Bech's car. He and the writer's wife were seated on the tier behind Bech. Two women, one a girl in her teens and the other a heavy old blonde, perhaps her mother, both dressed identically in sequined silver, did a hypnotic, languorous act with tinted pigeons, throwing them up in the air, watching them wheel through the shadows of the night club, and holding out their wrists for their return. They juggled with the pigeons, passed them between their legs, and for a climax the elderly blonde fed an aquamarine pigeon with seeds held in her mouth and fetched, one by one, on to her lips. 'Czechs,' Petrescu explained. The master of ceremonies reappeared in a blue wig and a toreador's jacket, and did a comic act with the dwarf, who had been fitted with papier-mâché horns. An East German girl, flaxen-haired and apple-cheeked, with the smooth columnar legs of the very young, came to the microphone dressed in a minimal parody of a cowgirl outfit and sang, in English, 'Dip in the Hot of Texas' and 'Allo Cindy Lou, Gootbye Hot'. She pulled guns from her hips and received much pro-American applause, but Bech was on his third Scotch and needed his hands to hold cigarettes. The Rumanian writer sat at the table beside him, a carafe of vodka at his elbow, staring stolidly at the floor show. He looked like the young Theodore Roosevelt, or perhaps McGeorge Bundy. His wife leaned forward and said in Bech's ear, 'Is just like home, hey? Texas is ringing bells?' He decided she was being sarcastic. A fat man in a baggy maroon tuxedo set up a long table and kept eight tin plates twirling on the ends of flexible sticks. Bech thought it was miraculous, but the man was booed. A touching black-haired girl from Bulgaria hesitantly sang three atonal folk songs into a chastened silence. Three women behind Bech began to chatter hissingly. Bech turned to rebuke them and was stunned by the size of their wristwatches, which were mansized, as in Russia. Also, in turning he had surprised Petrescu and the writer's wife holding hands. Though it was after midnight, the customers were still coming in, and the floor show refused to stop. The Polish girls returned dressed as ponies and jumped through hoops the dwarf held for them. The master of ceremonies reappeared in a striped bathing suit and black wig and did an act with the dwarf involving a stepladder and a bucket of water. A black dancer from Ghana twirled firebrands in the dark while slapping the floor with her bare feet. Four Latvian tumblers performed on a trampoline and a seesaw. The Czech mother and daughter came back in different costumes, spangled gold, but performed the identical act, the pigeons whirring, circling, returning, eating from the mother's lips. Then five Chinese girls from Outer Mongolia –

'My God,' Bech said, 'isn't this ever going to be over? Don't you Communists ever get tired of having fun?'

The writer's wife told him, 'For your money, you really gets.'

Petrescu and she conferred and decided it was time to go. One of the big wristwatches behind Bech said two o'clock. In leaving, they had to pass around the Chinese girls, who, each clad in a snug beige bikini, were concealing and revealing their bodies amid a weave of rippling coloured flags. One of the girls glanced sideways at Bech, and he blew her a pert kiss, as if from a train window. Their yellow bodies looked fragile to him; he felt that their bones, like the bones of birds, had evolved hollow, to save weight. At the mouth of the cave, the effeminate master of ceremonies, wearing a parrot headdress, was conferring with the hat-check girl. His intent was plainly heterosexual; Bech's head reeled at such duplicity. Though they added the weight of his coat to him, he rose like a balloon up the yellow stairs, bumped out through the green door, and stood beneath the street lamp inhaling volumes of the blue Rumanian night.

He felt duty-bound to confront the other writer.

They stood, the two of them, on the cobbled pavement, as if on opposite sides of a transparent wall one side of which was lacquered with Scotch and the other with vodka. The other's rimless glasses were misted and the resemblance to Teddy Roosevelt had been dissipated. Bech asked him, 'What do you write about?'

The wife, patting her nose with a handkerchief and struggling not to cough, translated the question, and the answer, which was brief. 'Peasants,' she told Bech. 'He wants to know, what do *you* write about?'

Bech spoke to him directly. '*La bourgeoisie*,' he said; and that completed the cultural exchange. Gently bumping and rocking, the writer's car took Bech back to his hotel, where he fell into the deep, unapologetic sleep of the sated.

The plane to Sofia left Bucharest the next morning. Petrescu and the ashen-faced chauffeur came into the tall *fin-de-siècle* dining-room for Bech while he was still eating breakfast – *jus d'orange, des croissants avec du beurre* and *une omelette aux fines herbes*. Petrescu explained that the driver had gone back to the theatre, and waited until the ushers and the managers left, after midnight. But the driver did not seem resentful, and gave Bech, in the sallow morning light, a fractional smile, a *risus sardonicus*, in which his eyes did not participate. On the way to the airport, he scattered a flock of chickens an old woman was coaxing across the road, and forced a military transport truck on to the shoulder, while its load of soldiers gestured and jeered. Bech's stomach grovelled, bathing the fine herbs of his breakfast in acid. The ceaseless tapping of the horn seemed a gnawing on all of his nerve ends. Petrescu made a fastidious mouth and sighed through his nostrils. 'I regret,' he said, 'that we did not make more occasion to discuss your exciting contemporaries.'

'I never read them. They're too exciting,' Bech said, as a line of uniformed schoolchildren was narrowly missed, and a field-worker with a wheelbarrow shuffled to safety, spilling potatoes. The day was overcast above the loamy sunken fields and the roadside trees in their skirts of white paint. 'Why,' he asked, not having meant to be rude, 'are all these tree trunks painted?'

'So they are,' Petrescu said, 'I have not noticed this before, in all my years. Presumably it is a measure to defeat the insects.'

The driver spoke in Rumanian, and Petrescu told Bech, 'He says it is for the car headlights, at night. Always he is thinking about his job.'

At the airport, all the Americans were there who had tried to meet Bech four days ago. Petrescu immediately delivered to Phillips, like a bribe, the name of the writer they had met last night, and Phillips said to Bech, 'You spent the evening with *him*? That's fabulous. He's the top of the list, man. We've never laid a finger on him before; he's been inaccessible.'

'Stocky guy with glasses?' Bech asked, shielding his eyes. Phillips was so pleased it was like a bright light too early in the day.

'That's the boy. For our money he's the hottest Red writer this side of Solzhenitsyn. He's *waaay* out. Stream of consciousness, no punctuation, everything. There's even some sex.'

'You might say he's Red hot,' Bech said.

'Huh? Yeah, that's good. Seriously, what did he say to you?

'He said he'll defect to the West as soon as his shirts come back from the laundry.'

'And we went,' Petrescu said, 'to La Caverne Bleue.'

'Say,' Phillips said, 'you really went underground.'

'I think of myself,' Bech said modestly, 'as a sort of low-flying U-2.'

'All kidding aside, Henry' – and here Phillips took Bech by the arms and squeezed – 'it sounds as if you've done a sensational job for us. Sensational. Thanks, friend.'

Bech hugged everyone in parting – Phillips, the chargé d'affaires, the junior chargé d'affaires, the ambassador's twelve-year-old nephew, who was taking archery lessons near the airport and had to be dropped off. Bech saved Petrescu for last, and walloped his back, for the man had led him to remember, what he was tempted to forget in America, that reading can be the best part of a man's life.

'I'll send you razor blades,' he promised, for in the embrace Petrescu's beard had scratched.

'No, no, I already buy the best. Send me books, any books!'

The plane was roaring to go, and only when safely, or fatally, sealed inside did Bech remember the chauffeur. In the flurry of formalities and baggage handling there had been no good-bye. Worse, there had been no tip. The leu notes Bech had set aside were still folded in his wallet, and his start of guilt gave way, as the runways and dark fields tilted and dwindled under him, to a vengeful satisfaction and glad sense of release. Clouds blotted out the country. He realized that for four days he had been afraid. The man next to him, a portly Slav whose bald brow was beaded with apprehensive sweat, turned and confided something unintelligible, and Bech said, '*Pardon, je ne comprends pas. Je suis Américain.*'

Appendix A

We are grateful for permission to reprint corroborating excerpts from the unpublished Russian journal of Henry Bech. The journal, physically, is a faded red Expenses diary, measuring 7⅜" by 4¼", stained by Moscow brandy and warped by Caucasian dew. The entries, of which the latter are kept in red ballpoint pen, run from 20 October 1964 to 6 December 1964. The earliest are the fullest.

I

20 Oct. Flight from NY at midnight, no sleep, Pan Am kept feeding me. Beating against the sun, soon dawn. Paris strange passing through by bus, tattered tired sepia sets of second-rate opera being wheeled through, false cheer of café awnings, waiting for chorus of lamp-lighters. Orly to Le Bourget. Moscow plane a new world. Men in dark coats waiting bunched. Solemn as

gangsters. Overheard first understood Russian word, *Americanski*, pronounced with wink towards me by snaggle-toothed gent putting bulky black coat in overhead rack. Rack netted cord, inside ribs of plane show, no capitalist plastic. Stewardesses not our smoothly extruded tarts but hefty flesh; served us real potatoes, beef sausage, borsch. Aeroflot a feast afloat. Crowded happy stable smell, animal heat in cold stable, five miles up. Uncles' back rooms in Wmsburg. Babble around me, foreign languages strangely soothing, at home in Babel. Fell asleep on bosom of void, grateful to be alive, home. Woke in dark again. Earth's revolution full in my face. Moscow dim on ocean of blackness, delicate torn veil, shy of electricity, not New York, that rude splash. Premonition: no one will meet. Author Disappears Behind Iron Curtain. Bech Best Remembered for Early Work. A delegation with roses waiting for me on other side of glass pen, wait for hours, on verge of Russia, decompressing, time different here, steppes of time, long dully lit terminal, empty of ads. Limousine driven by voiceless back of head, sleigh driver in Tolstoy, long haul to Moscow, a wealth of darkness, grey birches, slim, young, far from gnarled American woods. In hotel spelled out этáж waiting for elevator, French hidden beneath the Cyrillic. Everywhere, secrets.

II

23 Oct. Met Sobaka, head of Writers' U. Building Tolstoy's old manse, dining-room baronial oak. Litterateurs live like aristocrats. Sobaka has lipless mouth, wild bark, must have strangled men with bare hands. Tells me long story of love of his poetry expressed by coalminers in the Urals. Skip translating: '. . . then, here in . . . the deepest part of the mine . . . by only the light of, uh, carbon lights in the miners' caps . . . for three hours I recited . . . from the works of my youth, lyrics of the fields and forests of Byelorussia. Never have I known such enthusiasm. Never have I possessed such inspiration, such, ah, powers of memory. At the end . . . they wept to see me depart . . . these simple miners . . . their coal-blackened faces streaked, ah, veined with the silver of tears.'

'Fantastic,' I say.

'*Fantastichni*,' Skip translates.

Sobaka makes Skip ask me if I like the image, their faces of coal veined with silver.

'It's good,' say I.

'*Korosho*,' says Skip.

'The earth weeps precious metal,' I say. 'The world's working people weep at the tyranny of capital.'

Skip guffaws but translates, and Sobaka reaches under table and seizes my thigh in murderous pinch of conspiracy.

12 Nov. Back in Moscow, lunch at W.U. Sobaka in fine form, must have chopped off somebody's index finger this morning. Says trip to Irkutsk hazardous, airport might get snowed in. Hee hee hee. Suggests Kazakhstan instead, I say why not? – *nichyoo*. Eyeball to eyeball. He toasts Jack London, I toast Pushkin. He does Hemingway, I do Turgenev. I do Nabokov, he counters with John Reed. His mouth engulfs the glass and crunches. I think of what my dentist would say, my beautiful gold caps . . .

19 Nov. . . . I ask Kate where Sobaka is, she pretends not to hear. Skip tells me later he was friend of Khrush., hung on for while, now non-person. I miss him. My strange weakness for cops and assassins: their sense of craftsmanship?

III

1 Nov. Off to Caucasus with Skip, Mrs R., Kate. Fog, no planes for twenty-four hours. Airport crammed with

hordes of sleeping. Soldiers, peasants, an epic patience. Sleeping on clothy heaps of each other, no noise of complaint. Many types of soldier uniform, long coats. Kate after twelve hours bullies way on to plane, pointing to me as Guest of the State, fierce performance. Engines screaming, officials screaming, she screaming. Get on plane at 2 a.m., amid bundles, chickens, gypsies, sit opposite pair of plump fortune tellers who groan and (very discreetly) throw up all the way to Tbilisi. Ears ache in descent; no pressurization. Birds in airport, in and out, remind of San Juan. Happy, sleepless. Sun on hills, flowers like oleanders. Hotel as in Florida Keys in Bogart movies, sour early morning service, a bracing sense of the sinister. Great fist-shaking Lenin statue in traffic circle. Flies buzz in room.

2 Nov. Slept till noon. Reynolds wakes with phone call. He and Mrs caught later plane. Cowboys and Indians, even my escorts have escorts. We go in two cars to Pantheon on hill, Georgian escort lantern-jawed professor of aesthetics. Cemetery full of funny alphabet, big stone he says with almost tear in eye called simply 'Mother'. Reynolds clues me sotto voce it's Stalin's mother. Had been statue of S. here so big it killed two workmen when they pulled it down. Supper with many Georgian poets, toasts in white wine, my own keep calling them 'Russians' which Kate corrects in translation

to 'Georgians'. Author of epic infatuated with Mrs R., strawberry blonde from Wisconsin, puts hands on thighs, kisses throat, Skip grins sheepishly, what he's here for, to improve relations. Cable car down the mountain, Tbilisi a-spangle under us, all drunk, singing done in pit of throat, many vibrations, hillbilly mournfulness, back to bed. Same flies buzz.

3 Nov. Car ride to Muxtyeta, oldest church in Christendom, professor of aesthetics ridicules God, chastity, everybody winces. Scaldingly clear blue sky, church a ruddy octagonal ruin with something ancient and pagan in the centre. Went to lunch with snowy-haired painter of breasts. These painters of a sleazy ethnic softness, of flesh like pastel landscapes, landscapes like pastel flesh. Where are the real artists, the cartoonists who fill *Krokodil* with fanged bankers and cadaverous Adenauers, the anonymous Chardins of industrial detail? Hidden from me, like missile sites and working ports. Of the Russian cake they give me only frosting. By train to Armenia. We all share a four-bunk sleeper. Ladies undress below me, see Kate's hand dislodge beige buttoned canvasy thing, see circlet of lace flick past Ellen Reynolds's pale round knee. Closeted with female flesh and Skip's supercilious snore expect to stay awake, but fall asleep in top bunk like child among nurses. Yerevan station at dawn. The

women, puffy-eyed and mussed, claim night of total insomnia. Difficulty of women sleeping on trains, boats, where men are soothed. Distrust of machinery? Sexual stimulation, Claire saying she used to come just from sitting on vibrating subway seat, never the IRT, only the IND. Took at least five stops.

4 Nov. Svartz-Notz. Armenian cathedral. Old bones in gold bands. Our escort has withered arm, war record, dear smile, writing long novel about 1905 uprising. New city pink and mauve stone, old one Asiatic heaped rubble. Ruins of Alexander's palace, passed through on way to India. Gorgeous gorge.

5 Nov. Lake Sevan, grim grey sulphuric beach, lowered lake six feet to irrigate land. Land dry and rosy. Back at hotel, man stopped in lobby, recognized me, here from Fresno visiting relatives, said he couldn't finish *The Chosen*, asked for autograph. Dinner with Armenian science fiction writers, Kate in her element, they want to know if I know Ray Bradbury, Marshall McLuhan, Vance Packard, Mitchell Wilson. I don't. Oh. I say I know Norman Podhoretz and they ask if he wrote *Naked and Dead*.

6 Nov. Long drive to 'working' monastery. Two monks live in it. Chapel carved from solid rock, bushes full of

little strips of cloth, people make a wish. Kate borrows my handkerchief, tears off strip, ties to bush, makes a wish. Blushes when I express surprise. Ground littered with sacrificial bones. In courtyard band of farmers having ceremonial cookout honouring birth of son. Insist we join them, Reynoldses tickled pink, hard for American diplomats to get to clambake like this, real people. Priest scruffy sly fellow with gold fangs in beard. Armenians all wearing sneakers, look like Saroyan characters. Flies in wine, gobbets of warm lamb, blessings, toasts heavily directed towards our giggling round-kneed strawberry-blonde Ellen R. As we left we glimpsed real monk, walking along tumbledown parapet. Unexpectedly young. Pale, expressionless, very remote. A spy? Dry lands make best saints. Reynoldses both sick from effects of peoples' feast, confined to hotel while Kate and I, hardened sinners, iron stomachs, go to dinner with white-haired artist, painter of winsome faces, sloe eyes, humanoid fruit, etc.

7 Nov. Woke to band music; today Revolution Day. Should be in Red Square, but Kate talked me out of it. Smaller similar parade here, in square outside hotel. Overlooking while eating breakfast of blini and caviar parade of soldiers, red flags, equipment enlarging phallically up to rockets, then athletes in different colours

like gumdrops, swarm at end of children, people, citizens, red dresses conspicuous. Kate kept clucking tongue and saying she hates war. Reynoldses still rocky, hardly eat. Ellen admires my digestive toughness, I indifferent to her praise. Am I falling in love with Kate? Feel insecure away from her side, listen to her clear throat and toss in hotel room next to me. We walk in sun, I jostle to get between her and withered arm, jealous when they talk in Rooski, remember her blush when she tied half my torn hanky to that supernatural bush. What was her wish? Time to leave romantic Armenia. Back to Moscow by ten, ears ache fearfully in descent. Bitter cold, dusting of snow. Napoleon trembles.

IV

This sample letter, never sent, was found enclosed in the journal. 'Claire' appears to have been the predecessor, in Bech's affections, of Miss Norma Latchett. Reprinted by permission, all rights © Henry Bech.

Dear Claire:

I am back in Moscow, after three days in Leningrad, an Italian opera set begrimed by years in an arctic warehouse and populated by a million out-of-work baritone villains. Today, the American Ambassador gave me a dinner to which no Russians came, because of something they think we did in the Congo, and I spent the whole time discussing shoes with Mrs Ambassador, who hails originally, as she put it, from Charleston. She even took her shoe off so I could hold it – it was strange, warm, small. How are you? Can you feel my obsolete ardour? Can you taste the brandy? I live luxuriously, in the hotel where visiting plenipotentiaries from the Emperor of China are lodged, and Arabs in white robes leave oil trains down the hall. There may be an entire floor of English homosexual defectors, made over on the model of Cambridge digs. Lord, it's lonely, and bits of you – the silken depression beside each anklebone, the downy rhomboidal small of your back – pester me at night as I lie in exiled majesty, my laborious breathing being taped by three-score OGPU rookies. You were so beautiful. What happened? Was it all me, my fearful professional gloom, my Flaubertian syphilitic impotence? Or was it your shopgirl go-go brass, that held like a pornographic novel in a bureau (your left nipple was the drawer pull) a Quaker A-student from Darien? We turned each other inside out, it seemed to me, and made all those steak restaurants in the East Fifties light up like seraglios under bombardment. I will never be so young again. I am transported around here like a brittle curio;

plug me into the nearest socket and I spout red, white, and blue. The Soviets like me because I am redolent of the oppressive thirties. I like them for the same reason. You, on the other hand, were all sixties, a bath of sequins and glowing pubic tendrils. Forgive my unconscionable distance, our preposterous prideful parting, the way our miraculously synchronized climaxes came to nothing, like novae. Oh, I send you such airmail lost love, Claire, from this very imaginary place, the letter may beat the plane home, and jump into your refrigerator, and nestle against the illuminated parsley as if we had never said unforgivable things.

H.

Folded into the letter, as a kind of postscript, a picture postcard. On the obverse, in bad colour, a picture of an iron statue, male. On the reverse, this message:

Dear Claire: What I meant to
say in my unsent letter was that
you were so good to me, good for
me, there was a goodness in me you
brought to birth. Virtue is so rare,
I thank you forever. The man on the
other side is Mayakovsky, who shot
himself and thereby won Stalin's un-
dying love. Henry

John Updike

Gay with Sputnik stamps, it passed through the mails uncensored and was waiting for him when he at last returned from his travels and turned the key of his stifling, airless, unchanged apartment. It lay on the floor, strenuously cancelled. Claire had slipped it under the door. The lack of any accompanying note was eloquent. They never communicated again, though for a time Bech would open the telephone directory to the page where her number was encircled and hold it on his lap. — ED.

Appendix B

I. Books by Henry Bech (b. 1923, d. 19 –)

Travel Light, novel. New York: The Vellum Press, 1955.
London: J. J. Goldschmidt, 1957.

Brother Pig, novella. New York: The Vellum Press, 1957.
London: J. J. Goldschmidt, 1958.

When the Saints, miscellany. [*Contents*: 'Uncles and Dybbuks', 'Subway Gum', 'A Vote For Social Unconsciousness', 'Soft-Boiled Sergeants', 'The Vanishing Wisecrack', 'Graffiti', 'Sunsets Over Jersey', 'The *Arabian Nights* At Your Own Pace', 'Orthodoxy and Orthodontics', 'Rag Bag' [collection of book reviews], 'Displeased in the Dark' [collection of cinema reviews], forty-three untitled paragraphs under the head of 'Tumblers Clicking'.] New York: The Vellum Press, 1958.

The Chosen, novel. New York: The Vellum Press, 1963.
London: J. J. Goldschmidt, 1963.

The Best of Bech, anthology. London: J. J. Goldschmidt, 1968. [Contains *Brother Pig* and selected essays from *When the Saints*.]

Think Big, novel. New York: The Vellum Press, 1979. London: J. J. Goldschmidt, 1980.

2. Uncollected Articles and Short Stories

'Stee-raight'n Yo' Shoulduhs, Boy!', *Liberty*, XXXIV.33 (21 August 1943), 62–3.

'Home for Hannukah', *Saturday Evening Post*, CCXVII.2 (8 January 1944), 45–6, 129–33.

'Kosher Konsiderations', *Yank*, IV.4 (26 January 1944), 6.

'Rough Crossing', *Collier's*, XLIV (22 February 1944), 23–5.

'London Under Buzzbombs', *New Leader*, XXVII.11 (11 March 1944), 9.

'The Cockney Girl', *Story*, XIV.3 (May–June 1944), 68–75.

'V-Mail from Brooklyn', *Saturday Evening Post*, CCXVII.-25 (31 June 1944), 28–9, 133–7.

'Letter from Normandy', *New Leader*, XXVII.29 (15 July 1944), 6.

'Hey, Yank!', *Liberty*, XXXV.40 (17 September 1944), 48–9.

'Letter from the Bulge', *New Leader*, XXVIII.1 (3 January 1945), 6.

'Letter from the Reichstag', *New Leader*, XXVIII.23 (9 June 1945), 4.

'Fräulein, kommen Sie hier, bitte', *The Partisan Review*, XII (October 1945), 413–31.

'Rubble' [poem], *Tomorrow*, IV.7 (December 1945), 45.

'Soap' [poem], *The Nation*, CLXII (22 June 1946), 751.

'Ivan in Berlin', *Commentary*, I.5 (August 1946), 68–77.

'Jig-a-de-Jig', *Liberty*, XXVII.47 (15 October 1946), 38–9.

'Novels from the Wreckage', *New York Times Book Review*, LII (19 January 1947), 6.

☞ *The bulk of Bech's reviews, articles, essays, and prose-poems 1947–58 were reprinted in* When the Saints (*see above*). *Only exceptions are listed below.*

'My Favorite Reading in 1953', *New York Times Book Review*, LXVII (25 December 1953), 2.

'Smokestacks' [poem], *Poetry*, LXXXIV.5 (August 1954), 249–50.

'Larmes d'huile' [poem], *Accent*, XV.4 (Autumn 1955), 101.

'Why I Will Vote for Adlai Stevenson Again' [part of paid political advertisement printed in various newspapers], October 1956.

'My Favorite Salad', *McCall's*, XXXIV.4 (April 1957), 88.

'Nihilistic? Me?' [interview with Lewis Nichols], *New York Times Book Review*, LXI (12 October 1957), 17–18, 43.

'Rain King for a Day', *New Republic*, CXL.3 (19 January 1959), 22–3.

'The Eisenhower Years: Instant Nostalgia', *Esquire*, LIV.8 (August 1960), 51–4.

'Lay Off, Norman', *The New Republic*, CXLI.22 (14 May 1960), 19–20.

'Bogie: The Tic That Told All', *Esquire*, LV.10 (October 1960), 44–5, 108–111.

'The Landscape of Orgasm', *House and Garden*, XXI.3 (December, 1960), 136–41.

'Superscrew', *Big Table*, II.3 (Summer, 1961), 64–79.

'The Moth on the Pin', *Commentary*, XXXI (March 1961), 223–4.

'Iris and Muriel and Atropos', *New Republic*, CXLIV.20 (15 May 1961), 16–17.

'M-G-M and the USA', *Commentary*, XXXII (October 1961), 305–316.

'My Favorite Christmas Carol', *Playboy*, VIII.12 (December 1961), 289.

'The Importance of Beginning with a B: Barth, Borges, and Others', *Commentary*, XXXIII (February 1962), 136–42.

'Down in Dallas' [poem], *New Republic*, CXLVI.49 (2 December 1963), 28.

'My Favorite Three Books of 1963', *New York Times Book Review*, LXVII (19 December 1963), 2.

'Daniel Fuchs: An Appreciation', *Commentary*, XLI.2 (February 1964), 39–45.

'Silence', *The Hudson Review*, XVII (Summer 1964), 258–75.

'Rough Notes from Tsardom', *Commentary*, XLI.2 (February 1965), 39–47.

'Frightened Under Kindly Skies' [poem], *Prairie Schooner*, XXXIX.2 (Summer 1965), 134.

'The Eternal Feminine As It Hits *Me*' [contribution to a symposium], *Rogue*, III.2 (February 1966), 69.

'What Ever Happened to Jason Honeygale?' *Esquire*, LXI.9 (September 1966), 70–73, 194–8.

'Romanticism Under Truman: A Reminiscence', *New American Review*, III (April 1968), 59–81.

'My Three Least Favorite Books of 1968', *Book World*, VI (20 December 1968), 13.

3. Critical Articles Concerning (Selected List)

Prescott, Orville, 'More Dirt', *New York Times*, 12 October 1955.

Weeks, Edward, '*Travel Light* Heavy Reading', *Atlantic Monthly*, CCI.10 (October 1955), 131–2.

Kirkus Service, Virginia, 'Search for Meaning in Speed', XXIV (11 October 1955).

Time, 'V-v-vrooom!', LXXII.17 (12 October 1955), 98.

Macmanaway, Fr. Patrick X., 'Spiritual Emptiness Found

Behind Handlebars', *Commonweal*, LXXII.19 (12 October 1955), 387–8.

Engels, Jonas, 'Consumer Society Burlesqued', *Progressive*, XXI.35 (20 October 1955), 22.

Kazin, Alfred, 'Triumphant Internal Combustion', *Commentary*, XXIX (December 1955), 90–96.

Time, 'Puzzling Porky', LXXIV.3 (19 January 1957), 75.

Hicks, Granville, 'Bech Impressive Again', *Saturday Review*, XLIII.5 (30 January 1957), 27–8.

Callaghan, Joseph, S.J., 'Theology of Despair Dictates Dark Allegory', *Critic*, XVII.7 (8 February 1957), 61–2.

West, Anthony, 'Oinck, Oinck', *New Yorker*, XXXIII.4 (14 March 1957), 171–3.

Steiner, George, 'Candide as Schlemiel', *Commentary*, XXV (March 1957), 265–70.

Maddocks, Melvin, 'An Unmitigated Masterpiece', *New York Herald Tribune Book Review*, 6 February 1957.

Hyman, Stanley Edgar, 'Bech Zeroes In', *New Leader*, XLII.9 (1 March 1957), 38.

Poore, Charles, 'Harmless Hodgepodge', *New York Times*, 19 August 1958.

Marty, Martin, 'Revelations Within the Secular', *Christian Century*, LXXVII (20 August 1958), 920.

Aldridge, John, 'Harvest of Thoughtful Years', Kansas City *Star*, 17 August 1958.

Time, 'Who Did the Choosing?' LXXXIII.26 (24 May 1963), 121.

Klein, Marcus, 'Bech's Mighty Botch', *Reporter*, XXX.13 (23 May 1963), 54.

Thompson, John, 'So Bad It's Good', *New York Review of Books*, II.14 (15 May 1963), 6.

Dilts, Susan, 'Sluggish Poesy, Murky Psychology', Baltimore *Sunday Sun*, 20 May 1963.

Miller, Jonathan, 'Oopsie!', *Show*, III.6 (June 1963), 49–52.

Macdonald, Dwight, 'More in Sorrow', *Partisan Review*, XXVIII (Summer 1963), 271–9.

Kazin, Alfred, 'Bech's Strange Case Reopened', *Evergreen Review*, VII.7 (July 1963), 19–24.

Podhoretz, Norman, 'Bech's Noble Novel: A Case Study in the Pathology of Criticism', *Commentary*, XXXIV (October 1963), 277–86.

Gilman, Richard, 'Bech, Gass, and Nabokov: The Territory Beyond Proust', *Tamarack Review*, XXXIII.1 (Winter 1963), 87–99.

Minnie, Moody, 'Myth and Ritual in Bech's Evocations of Lust and Nostalgia', *Wisconsin Studies in Contemporary Literature*, V.2 (Winter Spring 1964), 1267 79.

Terral, Rufus, 'Bech's Indictment of God', *Spiritual Rebels in Post-Holocaustal Western Literature*, ed. Webster Schott (Las Vegas: University of Nevada Press, 1964).

L'Heureux, Sister Marguerite, 'The Sexual Innocence of Henry Bech', *America*, CX (11 May 1965), 670–74.

Brodin, Pierre, 'Henri Bech, le juif réservé', *Écrivains Americains d'aujourd'hui* (Paris : N.E.D., 1965).

Elbek, Leif, 'Damer og dæmoni', *Vindrosen*, Copenhagen (January–February 1965), 67–72.

Wagenback, Dolf, 'Bechkritic und Bechwissenschaft', *Neue Rundschau*, Frankfurt am Main, September–January 1965–6), 477–81.

Fiedler, Leslie, '*Travel Light*: Synopsis and Analysis', *E-Z Outlines*, No. 403 (Akron, O.: Hand-E Student Aids, 1966).

Tuttle, L. Clark, 'Bech's Best Not Good Enough', *Observer* (London), 22 April 1968.

Steinem, Gloria, 'What Ever Happened to Henry Bech?', *New York* II.46 (14 November 1969), 17–21.

a little history

Penguin Modern Classics were launched in 1961, and have been shaping the reading habits of generations ever since.

The list began with distinctive grey spines and evocative pictorial covers – a look that, after various incarnations, continues to influence their current design – and with books that are still considered landmark classics today.

Penguin Modern Classics have caused scandal and political change, inspired great films and broken down barriers, whether social, sexual or the boundaries of language itself. They remain the most provocative, groundbreaking, exciting and revolutionary works of the last 100 years (or so).

In 2011, on the fiftieth anniversary of the Modern Classics, we're publishing fifty Mini Modern Classics: the very best short fiction by writers ranging from Beckett to Conrad, Nabokov to Saki, Updike to Wodehouse. Though they don't take long to read, they'll stay with you long after you turn the final page.

MODERN CLASSICS
www.penguinclassics.com